Guide's Greatest

ESCAPE FROM CRIME STORIES

Greenwich SDA church
Pathfinder Club

Devonshire Drive
London
SE10 8JZ

Also by Helen Lee:

Guide's Greatest Prayer Stories
Guide's Greatest Miracle Stories
PowerGuide Logbook 2

To order, call 1-800-765-6955.
Visit us at www.rhpa.org for information on other Review and Herald products.

A special thanks to the authors we were unable to locate. If anyone can provide knowledge of their current mailing address, please relay this information to Helen Lee, in care of the Review and Herald Publishing Association, 55 West Oak Ridge Drive, Hagerstown, MD 21740.

HELEN LEE, editor

Guide's Greatest

ESCAPE FROM CRIME STORIES

REVIEW AND HERALD® PUBLISHING ASSOCIATION

Since 1861 | www.reviewandherald.com

The authors assume full responsibility for the accuracy of all facts
and quotations as cited in this book.

All Scripture references are from the *Holy Bible, New International Version*.
Copyright © 1973, 1978, 1984, International Bible Society. Used by per-
mission of Zondervan Bible Publishers.

This book was
Edited by Helen Lee
Cover Designed by Trent Truman
Cover art by Ralph Butler
Typeset: 13/16 Goudy

PRINTED IN U.S.A.

07   5 4 3 2

Library of Congress Cataloging-in-Publication Data
Lee, Helen. editor.
  Guide's greatest escape from crime stories / Helen Lee, editor.
     p. cm.
  ISBN 978-0-8280-1753-4
  1. Christian life—Juvenile works. 2. Crime—Juvenile works.
3. Children's stories. 4. Christian life. 5. Crime. 6. Short stories. I. Title.
PZ5 .G83 2003
818.6
                              2003271667

Introduction

A book on bandits and burglars? An unusual theme, I'll admit. And when someone first suggested it to me, I wasn't sure what the end result would be.

But thinking about the story of the Good Samaritan in the Bible, and also of Jesus' conversation with the thief on the cross, I began searching for stories of bandits and burglars in the pages of *Guide* (a weekly Christian magazine for young people). What I discovered was a wide array of exciting, wonderful stories, including:

- miracle stories
- angel stories
- stories of answered prayer
- conversion stories
- stories of God's protection
- and reminders of Jesus' second coming

I hope you enjoy reading the stories in this book. And my prayer is that you and I will be ready to meet Jesus when He comes again. God bless you.

—Helen Lee

Contents

1

A Dagger for a Bible

by Wayne E. Olson

The traveler looked around uneasily. He had come to a dangerous part of his journey. He must pass through Walnut Creek Canyon. Rock walls rose steep and forbidding on both sides, and the narrow, twisting path was covered with boulders. But it was not these that made him afraid. There were evil tales told about this canyon, tales of bandits, and of travelers robbed of all they carried. Sometimes people who entered this narrow gorge were never seen again.

Fortunately, there were still several hours before dark, and he should be well past the danger zone before the sun went down. He clutched his books a little tighter, and plunged into the canyon. But he did more than that, for Michael was a Bible salesman. He offered a silent prayer for the Lord's protection.

At first the path was easy enough, and his hurrying feet made good time. Michael was able to look at the scene around him and examine the canyon carefully. What an ominous place it was! Everywhere stood great rocks reaching high into the air, some by themselves, others in groups. Magnificent hiding places, he observed. Worse than that, some of these rocks stood right beside the trail. A bandit might hide behind one until a traveler was within inches, then step out and attack.

As he descended lower into the canyon, the path became narrower and more twisty. The rocks became more numerous, and it was with increasing difficulty that he found places for his feet. Soon he had to take his eyes away from observing the hiding places, and concentrate on the path. *Oh, well,* Michael thought, *I know this canyon has a bad reputation, but I've been through it many times without harm.*

"Stop, or I'll kill you!" a voice suddenly rang out.

Startled, Michael looked up. There, right in front of him, stood a masked bandit, a curved dagger upraised in his right hand, ready to strike.

Michael stopped.

The bandit continued, only his eyes showing above his mask. "First hand me all your money," he demanded. "Then I am going to kill you."

There was nothing hurried or excited in the bandit's tone. He sounded as though he was doing something he had done many times before, and fully intended to do again.

Michael looked at him steadily. This was a time for quick thinking. One mistake would cost him his life, and he didn't want to die right then. *Should I defy the bandit?* he wondered. That would be risky indeed. *Should I try to fight him?* A sudden leap to catch the bandit's arm, with a hard slam to his face, might take him off guard and save the Bible salesman's life. Most people would have said that this was his only chance.

But Michael decided on another method of defense. He made up his mind he would treat the bandit the way he believed Jesus would have.

Speaking as kindly as he could, he said quietly, "Friend, I haven't much money, but I will give it to you." He held out his purse.

If the bandit was surprised, he did not show it. The knife was still held menacingly.

"And if you want to kill me," Michael went on, "I will not object. But I will feel very sorry for you if you kill me. You see, I am ready to die. If you kill me it won't hurt much, for I shall have eternal life. But I am grieved to think how much it will hurt you."

The bandit did not know what to say. He had never heard anyone talk like this.

"I shall be sorry for you," Michael continued, "because of all the suffering you will endure. In the first place, as soon as you kill me, you will be a hunted man. The police will be after you. You will never again be able to return home without the constant fear that you will be arrested and hanged for your crime. In the second place, even if the police don't catch you right away, your conscience will condemn you. You will never be peaceful or happy again, for you will know that you have broken God's law. And then, when you die, as die you must, you will have to meet God, and you won't know how to answer Him. I, however, am ready to go peacefully and unafraid."

The bandit stood speechless, his arm slowly dropping. Finally he found his voice. "Where, where," he stammered, "did you find out how to die without being afraid? I have killed other men, and they were always frightened. I would be afraid to die, just as you have said."

Michael reached under his coat and brought out his Bible. "In here," he said. He turned to one of his favorite texts and read, "Even though I walk through the valley of the shadow of death, I will fear no evil, for you are with me {Psalm 23:4}."

He turned to another. "'Blessed are you when people . . . persecute you . . . because of me. Rejoice and be glad, because great is your reward in heaven' {Matthew 5:11, 12}."

"Does it really say that?" the bandit interrupted.

"Oh, yes. Listen to this: 'Though your sins are like scarlet, they shall be as white as snow; though they are red as crimson, they shall be like wool.' And this:

'If we confess our sins, he is faithful and just and will forgive us our sins and purify us from all unrighteousness' {Isaiah 1:18; 1 John 1:9}."

"Is that true?" asked the bandit, his voice trembling.

"It surely is."

"Do you believe it?"

"Yes."

"Would it apply to my sins? Would God forgive me?"

For a moment Michael didn't know whether the bandit was sincere or not. But as he looked into the bandit's eyes, he saw *tears!*

"Friend," Michael said, clasping the bandit's hand, "of course it's true. And you can have your sins forgiven. Would you—would you like us to kneel down right here and pray about it?"

"Please," the bandit replied in a faltering voice.

So there, on that rocky, narrow canyon trail, Michael and the bandit knelt side by side. You may call it amazing. There, on that path, with their arms about each other, Michael prayed for the man who only a few minutes earlier had wanted to kill him.

When they stood again, the bandit said to Michael, "May I have one of those Books?"

"You may have this one," said Michael. "But I do not want money for it. I want something else."

"What?"

"I would like to exchange this Bible for your dagger."

"That's fair enough," said the bandit. Then, as they made the exchange, the man who used to be a bandit said, "In case you think I was joking when I threatened to kill you, it will interest you to know that I have already killed seven men with this dagger, and I would just as soon have killed you along with the rest. But God stopped me, and I will never kill another."

When this story was printed, Michael was still selling books for God in Lebanon.

The Foolish Bandit

by Lawrence Maxwell

Mr. George Whitefield was one of the greatest evangelists of all time. One day, while he was traveling with a friend, someone told him about a widow whose furniture was about to be taken away from her unless she could pay a certain amount of money right away. Mr. Whitefield promptly gave her five guineas, about $14 now, but worth far more then.

As they continued their journey, the friend said, "You know you can't afford to give the widow all that money. Why did you do it?"

"When God brings a case of distress before us, He wants us to relieve it," Mr. Whitefield replied.

As they traveled on horseback, suddenly they saw a cloud of dust coming toward them from a hidden place. Then out of the dust emerged a masked man.

"Your money or your life," demanded the bandit,

threatening them with a pistol. Mr. Whitefield and his friend stopped and obligingly emptied their purses into the highwayman's hands. What else could they do?

The bandit left, and the two travelers continued on their way. "Now who do you think was wiser?" Mr. Whitefield asked his friend. "I gave my money to the widow, and it is doing her some good. You kept yours, and the bandit has it."

As far as we know, the friend made no reply. And about that time the men had other things to think about, for the sound of horse's hoofs behind startled them, and they turned around to see the bandit almost upon them again.

"Stop!" he ordered, waving his gun.

"What now, friend?" asked Mr. Whitefield.

"I want that coat you have on. It's nicer than mine."

"Very well," said Mr. Whitefield. He took off his good coat and handed it to the robber, who gave Mr. Whitefield his ragged coat in return.

Once again Mr. Whitefield and his friend continued their journey. They were nearing a village when for the third time they heard those galloping hoofs.

"He must want to kill us this time," the friend exclaimed. They struck spurs to their horses, making all haste to reach the safety of the town. The race continued pell-mell for several minutes until the bandit, seeing that he could not overtake the travelers before they would arrive at the village, gave up.

Later that night Mr. Whitefield took off the ragged old jacket the thief had given him. In one of the pockets, neatly wrapped, was a packet of coins worth 100 guineas, doubtless the gleanings of many holdups, and 20 times as much money as Mr. Whitefield had given the poor widow that morning!

3

Burglars in the Basement

by V. E. Robinson

Billy and Jack wandered along the streets of the small pioneer town in Western Colorado. They had come with their parents from their farm 18 miles away. They didn't have much money in their pockets, but they still enjoyed looking in the store windows.

What interested them the most that day was a picture they saw in the post office, which was located in a corner of the general store. While Father was getting the mail, Billy wandered over and looked at some pictures pasted to the wall.

"Look here, Jack," he called to his brother. "These are two men they're trying to catch: Scarface Al and Texas Sam. Bad men, this says they are, and wanted by the government. Scarface has a mark down one side of his face, and Sam has only three fingers on one hand. They held up a train over near Leadville, and took off solidly banked up for the winter. Here, help me, and I think we can fix them."

Billy yanked up the rag carpet covering the kitchen floor. He grabbed the ring and pulled the trapdoor open, laying it down flat on the floor. Then they spread the rug smoothly over the empty space, concealing the hole, and then anxiously waited for the robbers to return. In order to avert suspicion, Billy remained near the stove as if still busy making preparations for supper. Jack stood in the shadow near the living room door.

After what seemed like an hour, the boys heard the intruders returning. Down the stairs they came. They were in a very bad mood, for evidently they had not found as much loot as they had expected. The first man set the lantern down near the door and with his sack over his shoulder stepped into the kitchen, closely followed by his companion.

"Ha! Now for some supper," he exclaimed, "and see that you boys—" He got no further with that sentence. Stepping onto the edge of the rug concealing the opening, he went plunging down into the basement.

His companion halted suddenly, but a vigorous push from Jack caused him to lose his balance, and throwing up his hands, he too dropped through the hole. But as he fell, he managed to grasp the edge of the floor. Hanging on, he made desperate efforts to draw himself up.

Both boys grasped the trap door and slammed it

down, which caused the man to release his hold and drop to the bottom of the cellar with a cry of anguish. In the brief glimpse they had of his hands, however, Billy noted that one hand had only three fingers.

The boys dragged everything heavy they could find onto the trapdoor. They brought a big chest from the living room. The wood box followed, and then the boys sat on top of the boxes. They shuddered as they listened to the fearful language coming from the cellar. The boys had no appetite for supper.

Time seemed to drag by as they waited for sounds indicating the return of their father and mother. The clock on the wall slowly ticked off the minutes. Billy expressed the fear that their prisoners might dig their way out, but Jack assured him it was impossible.

It was nearly midnight when they heard the horses' steady trot coming up the driveway. "You go and tell them," Jack said. "I'm not going to leave this trapdoor."

Billy was away like a flash, stumbling down the steps, running to the wagon, shouting in the greatest excitement, "We've got 'em! The robbers. We've got 'em!"

It was some time before the astonished parents could really grasp the situation. Mother shuddered as she thought of what those bad men might have done to her boys. Father was unwilling to leave the men under his house an hour longer than necessary.

"Here, Mother," he said. "You watch the door. I'm

going for the sheriff."

On his fastest horse Mr. Brown raced back over the miles to town, and before the sun had climbed over the eastern mountains he was back with the sheriff and six men. They found Mrs. Brown sitting on the box over the trap door, having sent the boys off to bed with a promise to call them when the sheriff came.

The officer could hardly believe that two boys had really cornered the two wanted men, but had to admit it was true when the men sullenly climbed the cellar steps, hands held high in the air. Quickly the handcuffs were snapped on, and they started a long journey back to town.

Once again Father gathered his family together, and taking the big Bible, read the ninety-first Psalm. Then kneeling, he poured out his gratitude to God for His loving watch care over his children in their time of need.

The rest of the story is quickly told. Both robbers were sent up for long terms in the penitentiary. Billy and Jack collected the $500 and used most of it for their education. Throughout long lives, both continued to tell their children and grandchildren the story of the greatest adventure of their boyhood days.

4

The Prisoners Kept Singing

by Ka Le Paw and Eric B. Hare

It was a hot steamy day toward the end of the rainy season. A large canoe drifted down the river and stopped along the bank of the muddy Salween, carrying a group of men armed with long sharp knives and guns. They were bandits, feared and dreaded by the whole jungle.

It was the time of day when all the students were in school, and everybody else rested and slept. So no one was at the riverbank to give an alarm.

Leaving two men in charge of the canoe, the bandits sprang to the shore and quietly followed their chief along the trail toward the village. As the schoolhouse came into view, the bandit chief paused and said, "There it is, boys. It's full of teachers and students, and not a knife or a gun among them. Surround the building quietly, and when I shoot they will all scream and run for the jungle. Catch as many as you can. People who can send their children to school have money, and we should get enough ransom out of this to see us comfortably through a month or two."

Bang! went the bandit's gun.

Pastor Chit Maung glanced out the window and saw the group of armed bandits that surrounded the school. His face paled, and it was hard to talk, but he managed to exclaim, "It's bandits! Try your best to run for the jungle."

Down the steps ran the students, many of them screaming with fear.

"Only the biggest!" shouted the bandit chief. "They are worth more and easier to look after!"

"Thara Chit Maung, help!" screamed a 15-year-old boy as a robber held him fast.

"Keep quiet if you know what's good for you!" growled the bandit.

"Maung Thein, Maung Thein, where are you? Help!"

The next few moments were filled with terror. The news was quickly shouted throughout the village. Men, women, and mothers with their babies on their backs quickly stopped their work, left their cooking on the fire, and fled for their lives. It was just what the bandits wanted. No resistance, an empty village, and 10 prisoners from 15 to 22 years of age.

The prisoners were tied up and held under watch while the bandits carefully ransacked each bamboo house. All money, and any food and clothing they wanted, they carried away. As they led the prisoners and carried the loot to the large canoe at the river's edge, the bandit chief left a note under a stone at the side of the path: "In seven days, leave 25,000 rupees at this spot, and your friends will be released the next morning."

The village people and the school children nervously waited in the jungle until at last the scouts brought the news. "They're gone. They're gone! You can all come back now!" A roll call quickly revealed that four teachers and six students had been kidnapped.

There was little sleep for anyone that night. They were too afraid to lie down, and sat huddled in the darkness or around little fires. Here and there could be heard an occasional prayer, "O God, keep them safe. O God, keep them faithful."

The next day the friends and relatives of the kidnapped ones began putting together all the money they could find. They dug up bottles filled with their savings—paper money and silver rupees. They sold rice and other possessions they could do without, but try as they would, all they could come up with was 1,500 rupees—and the bandits had demanded 25,000 rupees! On the seventh night they left it by the rock

"'You don't?' said the robbers in surprise. 'After three weeks of plain rice and salt, you don't want something delicious to eat?'

"'The Bible says pigs and turtles are unclean, and we would rather have just rice and salt again.'

"The robbers couldn't believe their ears. 'Never heard of anything like this!'

"'They are the most unusual people in the world—don't smoke! don't drink! don't eat pork! don't eat turtle! Just sing, sing, sing!'

"'Well, what about a little fish to eat with your rice?'

"'Thank you, we would like that,' we said.

"Then they took us to the river, rowed us down in the large canoe a few miles, then let us go. And here we are, thank the dear Lord."

And thank the Lord they did. The next Sabbath afternoon was set aside in the Moulmein chapel as a special praise service. Each captive that was now free took part, told of his experience, and how it had strengthened his faith. Everyone was glad, and everyone praised God for the teachers and students who had been so true and faithful, and for their God who is "our refuge and strength, an ever-present help in trouble" (Psalm 46:1).

5

Thief on the Train

As told to Lois Christian Randolph

We had a strange experience on the train to Warsaw, Poland. It's really too bad that such a thing had to happen to Professor Howell. You see, last Monday, Elder Town, Professor Howell, and I were in a four-berth sleeping compartment on the train for Warsaw, Poland, where we had to attend some meetings. We planned to arrive in Warsaw at 7:00 Tuesday morning.

On Monday evening the conductor stopped by for our tickets. "You men should open the window more so you'll have some fresh air during the night," he suggested. He then opened the outside window about six inches.

After he left, we piled our suitcases against the door that opened into the long corridor that runs the full length of the sleeping cars. We wanted to be sure no one would get in and steal our things during the night. Then we got into bed.

Before 6:00 the next morning Professor Howell got up to dress and shave. "Where are they?" he exclaimed, fumbling around. "Who's been here? Is someone playing a joke on me? This can't have happened."

I was barely awake, but when I heard his remarks, a dreadful truth dawned on me. I sat up with a start. During the night, while the three of us had been sleeping, someone had stolen Professor Howell's clothes and his suitcases. We wondered if that was why the conductor had been so anxious for the window to be open.

"I'm going to have to walk along the streets of Warsaw in my pajamas," Professor Howell moaned.

Elder Town and I had lost nothing, and we tried to see what we could do to help this good man who had come all the way from America. I looked around and discovered that fortunately he had placed a package with his passport and billfold under his pillow—a wise precaution. He had not lost any money or traveler's checks. At the moment, however, I wondered if the thieves would not have been kinder if they had taken some of the money and left a few of his clothes. You see, Professor Howell was six feet seven inches tall!

"I don't have a garment on this side of the

Atlantic except the pajamas I am wearing," Professor Howell said.

We were in quite a dilemma. How could we get the professor off the train respectably dressed? The train would reach Warsaw in just 40 minutes!

Fortunately, I found Professor Howell's overcoat. He had used it as an extra blanket and hadn't noticed it when he turned back the covers in the morning. I felt like the hero of a great battle when I discovered that he did have that one garment. It would help so much in getting him off the train without embarrassment.

Professor Howell could not possibly wear any of my clothes, no matter how generous I felt. Elder Town was a bit taller than I, but only five feet 11 at that. He lent Professor Howell a pair of trousers, but they struck our tall brother about six inches above his ankles. It was the best we could do. Then we discovered that the thieves had overlooked a pair of shoes, and that helped too. Never before had an overcoat and a pair of shoes seemed like such a blessing.

Some brethren from the Polish Union Conference came down to the train to meet us. Soon we were in a taxi on our way to a hotel. In less than two hours the Polish brethren had two tailors in our hotel with samples of materials, ready to go into action.

Professor Howell was stuck in the hotel room for

three days, unable to go out while the suits were being made. Meals were no problem because the hotel provided room service. But he missed most of the meetings, and the story of his mishap got around.

Professor Howell didn't lament so much the loss of his clothes, but he was sad that all the notes he had taken while he was visiting the Adventist schools in Europe were gone. They had been in his briefcase. While the tailors worked, he did his best to reproduce from memory as many of the notes as possible.

Friday evening, in a new suit, Professor Howell preached a powerful sermon on the text, "But understand this: If the owner of the house had known at what time of night the thief was coming, he would have kept watch and would not have let his house be broken into. So you also must be ready, because the Son of Man will come at an hour when you do not expect him" (Matthew 24:43, 44). His stirring sermon reminded us to be sure that the second coming of Jesus does not take us by surprise.

6

The Disappearing Clothes

by Ida E. Roosenberg

Can we? Oh, can we, Dad?" I begged as I hopped around Dad's chair.

"Calm down, sis. Let Dad think," my brother, Hall, commanded.

"We-e-ell," Dad thoughtfully remarked after several more minutes of figuring. "I think we can swing it this spring."

I pranced about the room while Mom and my older sister, Lucile, bent their heads eagerly over the new spring catalog. Dad had just said that we could order some new clothes! What a thrill it was! For this was at the close of the Depression, when new things in our home were as rare as rags in a millionaire's palace.

"Mom, may I help pick the color of my new skirt?" I asked. "I want blue."

"Here are overalls like the ones I want," Hall said briefly.

After a great deal of rehashing, rejecting, and rejoicing, the order was ready for the mail. Never were days so long or so slow to pass as were those of the following week.

"Isn't it wonderful that the crops are doing so well that we can get new clothes?" I confided to our faithful collie, Pepper.

Day after day I raced to the mailbox only to turn back disappointed.

"Quit being so impatient!" Hall grumbled. "If you keep watching, it won't come."

Finally the package arrived! We gathered about it like children around a Christmas tree. With quivering fingers Lucile untied the endless knots. It was like having Christmas and all our birthdays combined, an ecstatic day indeed.

The following Monday morning Mom prepared to wash with the old hand washer. Tubs of water were bubbling on the stove, and the "knuckle knocker" scrubbing board was resting at the edge of the washer.

Mom sorted the dirty clothes. Today there weren't only ragged and worn clothes, but many new things being washed for the first time. "This is one day I'm glad to have a large washing," Mom mused as she carried the steaming water to the tubs.

"Ida, will you help hang up the clothes?" Mom asked. "You may hang these stockings on the low line next to the spirea bushes."

As I hung the stockings, drops of rain began to fall, presenting us with quite a problem! In those days dryers were unheard-of, and there were too many clothes to dry in the dining room on crisscross lines around the barrel shaped stove.

"Martin, what shall I do?" Mom asked Dad. "Should I leave the clothes outdoors overnight, hoping they'll dry tomorrow, or what?"

"I think it'll be all right," Dad said. And so Mom left the laundry on the lines. With the lulling lullaby of rain we soon went wearily to bed.

Mom was awakened in the wee hours of the morning by a noise outside. "Martin! Martin! I hear something! Wake up! Pepper's growling! Hurry!" whispered Mom.

Quickly Dad looked out all the windows and even went onto the kitchen steps and peered over the starless landscape, but he saw nothing unusual. "You must have been dreaming," he said to her as he crawled back into bed.

The next morning, kerosene lantern in hand, Dad and Hall sloshed through the mud to the barn. The mud caked on the cows made the chores a lengthy and tiresome process. But just as the sun began to filter through the porous sides of the barn, Hall threw the last forkful of hay into the manger.

"Done for another morning! And I'm sure glad, because I need to fix fences today," Dad said as he picked up two pails of milk and started for the house. "Hey, Hall! Where are all the clothes Mom washed yesterday? She hasn't taken them down yet, has she?"

Hall ran as rapidly as possible through the deep mud to the kitchen. "Mom! Mom! Where are all the clothes you washed?"

"Where I left them, of course—right on the line!"

"No, they aren't!"

"They have to be!"

We all ran out the kitchen door to view in shocked horror a scene of recent battle. There had definitely been a fight. Clothespins were thrown helter-skelter, and there were muddy tracks on the wet grass and clothes in bunches all over the ground.

"But, Mama," I whimpered, "these are only our old clothes on the ground. Where are the new ones?"

"I think we'll find them somewhere around here if we look," Dad said.

After looking in the hollyhocks, under the spirea bushes, and around the windmill, Mom concluded, "Evidently someone took our new clothes. Someone who knew we had them. Someone who knew I had left them out too. It looks as though Pepper tried to stop them, but didn't succeed. Well, come on in, and we'll have morning worship."

Dad admitted that Mom must be right as we dragged ourselves up the steps into the kitchen. Each one of us felt a special burden while offering our prayers through tear-choked voices. We asked the Lord to help us find our clothes and get them back.

In a stupor Hall and Lucile departed for school, Dad went to feed the chickens, and I left to play in the yard. I could hear Mom singing while she rolled out the dough for a batch of cookies.

All morning we tried to solve the mystery. Where had our clothes disappeared to? Did someone take them? How could we find them?

Meanwhile Dad finished feeding and watering the chickens and went to the barn. It was time to turn the cows out to pasture. "H'mmmm, that looks peculiar. I never saw a track like that before," he mumbled as he neared the barn.

Later, after turning the cows out to pasture, Dad's curiosity got the better of him, and he decided to follow the strange-looking tracks. They led to a deep dark spot under the barn that Pepper and her five puppies were calling home.

"Flossie! Flossie! Come quick!" Dad called.

Hurrying to the kitchen door, I yelled, "Mama! Mama! Dad wants you right away. Quick!"

"What is it? What's the matter?" Mom came out of the door, wiping her flour-covered hands.

Already Dad was at the barnyard gate calling,

"Come on out here with me a minute."

Dad began leading Mom toward the barn. I trailed behind like a puppy dog.

"What's wrong? Is the new cow sick?"

"No, the cow is all right, but I have some tracks to show you. See, there's an odd track in the mud. What would you say made it?"

"It looks as if Pepper has been dragging her puppies. Is that all you wanted me to see?"

"Much more than that!" Dad proclaimed. "Look closer!" He stepped forward, still grinning smugly. He pointed to a large man's bootprint near the clothesline, then another, and still another human track.

"Do you think Pepper had a fight with a man?" Mom asked.

"Yes. There must have been quite a struggle."

"Where's Pepper now?"

"Let's follow these dragging marks," suggested Dad, "and we'll see where they lead."

As they progressed, Pepper bounded from under the barn with a yelp, enthusiastically wagging her tail and looking up as though to say, "Don't you think I'm pretty good?"

"There," continued Dad. "Look at that thing protruding from under the barn."

Gingerly Mom bent over and reached for the muddy something. "Oh! Oh-h-h!" she gasped. "It's one of our new pillowcases! How did it get here? Are the rest of the clothes with it?"

"Yes, they're all here, all covered with mud. You can thank Pepper for saving them. She must have chased the thief away during the night. Perhaps afterward she brought the clothes out here as a safety precaution."

Bending over, Dad pulled out more and more clothes, and we joyfully gathered them into our arms.

Never had Pepper received such praise as we gave her then. And reaching the house, we knelt again and thanked God that we had our new clothes after all.

Once more the washtubs were filled. And this time I could hardly hear the swishy squeak of the old wringer, Mom was singing so loudly.

7

Clink-clank of Bandits' Guns

by William J. Harris

Chang Po Ching knew it was dangerous. He was on the wrong side of the line. War and commotion had made traveling perilous. And even though he was doing the Lord's work, he knew he was in bandit territory.

He had started out early that morning, sitting on a wheelbarrow and being pushed along. Wheelbarrow travel was slow at best, and Chang Po Ching wanted to get down to the church at Nan Tsun as soon as possible. It had been months since he had been there, and he wanted to help the colporteurs* as they went out to sell the Chinese *Signs of the Times*.

They had not traveled far when the barrow man stopped. "Those men on the road up ahead do not look like local farmers," he whispered.

"We cannot go back," Brother Chang said. "Let

us not appear frightened. We will proceed slowly and go on by, attending to our own business."

But the very next thing Chang Po Ching and his barrow man heard was, "Halt!" Rifles clink-clanked as they were brought into position!

"Who are you and where are you from?" one of the bandits demanded.

Chang Po Ching knew that it would be unwise to reveal that he was from across the lines. In hesitant language he explained that he was from "back up there," and gestured with his hand. He did not want to say he was from Peking. That would create even more problems.

"Where are you going?"

"Just down the road a ways," he replied.

"That's what I thought," blurted out the leader. "You're a spy!"

"No, honorable captain, I am no spy. I am a worker for the Jesus doctrine. I belong to the Jesus missions."

The bandits were not satisfied. "You are a spy. You claim to belong to the mission just so we will let you go."

"Take him out and shoot him," called the leader.

"No, please don't do that. I am a loyal Chinese. I love my country and am not a spy."

"Where did you get those leather shoes?" they demanded.

Ordinarily Chinese people wore shoes made of cloth. But church workers, who had to travel so much, often wore a foreign type of shoe made of leather. Chang Po Ching's leather shoes immediately alerted the bandits that he was not from around there in the farming country. Besides, he didn't walk like a farmer or talk like one. Obviously, he must be from the city.

"You are from Peking, aren't you?" the leader snarled.

"Yes," Chang Po Ching said, "I will admit that I am from Peking. But I am not a spy. I am a worker for the Jesus doctrine. I am a Christian young man. I am not a soldier and have never had any military service!"

In China there was a way to tell whether a person had military experience or not. Anyone who had been a soldier would have a rough and callused place on his shoulder from where a gun had rubbed week after week and month after month.

The bandits stepped closer to Chang Po Ching and tore off his upper garments. They felt his shoulder bone and skin. There were no calluses. The skin was smooth.

The men began to argue among themselves. Maybe he *was* a young preacher. Maybe he wasn't a spy. Perhaps they should not shoot him. And all this time Chang Po Ching was praying to know what to do next.

Then the leader spoke up. "Bind him up. We'll take him to the captain. If the captain says, 'Shoot him,' then we'll shoot him. Whatever the captain says goes!"

The bandits bound him tight and led him across the fields to their camp. It was early morning, and the sun was just coming up. Chang Po Ching was thinking all the way over there. What could he say? What could he do to prove that he was indeed a worker for the Jesus doctrine and not a spy? He prepared a speech as well as he could as he stumbled along on the plowed fields.

When they arrived at their destination, the captain was not up yet. The men awakened him, and he came out, sour-faced and angry. He was a large man with a hard, mean look on his face. Without giving Chang Po Ching an opportunity to make his speech, he scanned him up and down and shouted, "Take him out shoot him!"

"Honorable Captain," Chang Po Ching pleaded, "please, Your Honor, I am no spy. I am sure you know of the Christian religion. I am a Christian worker. I am a loyal Chinese. I tell my people about Jesus, the Son of heaven. I am a preacher of the Jesus doctrine."

"Line up your men, stand him up, and shoot him!"

So there was no way out. He must be shot. What could he do? What could he say? Bowing once more before the ruthless leader, Chang Po Ching said, "Your Honor, if I must die, will you permit me to read a bit from the Christian's Holy Book over there in my bundle?"

The captain turned and gruffly ordered a coolie soldier to untie his hands. Chang Po Ching reached down and picked up his Bible and leafed through it. Where were some of those promises? Where were those words of comfort? He was so nervous that the pages were all blurred to him. The rifles were going click, clank, clink as the men marched to the firing lines. He had only moments to live. Frantically he turned the pages. Ah, here was something. He read it out loud. "Do not let your hearts be troubled. . . . In my Father's house are many rooms. . . . I am going there to prepare a place for you. . . . I will come back and take you to be with me [John 14:1-3]."

Chang Po Ching felt his courage coming back. He looked up at the bandits. "This war," he said, "this trouble and commotion our country is in, means something. It means that Jesus, the Son of heaven, the Savior of the world, is coming again. He is coming back to this earth. My job is to tell my people of the great event. My work is to help my countrymen get ready for heaven."

Those rough men stood still and listened, amazed. They had never heard anything like this. Their mouths fell open. Even the haughty captain listened quietly. And Chang Po Ching continued for nearly a half hour, speaking with all the earnestness of his soul, preaching to those rough bandits about the coming of Jesus.

When he paused, the captain looked up. "Shoot that man?" he said. "No! We must not shoot a man like this. He surely is a Christian preacher. This is the very message our people need. Turn him loose! Let him go! We don't shoot men like him!"

And so the bandits turned him loose. He picked up his bundle, threw it over his shoulder, and went on down the road to the church where the colporteurs were meeting.

When he got down there he told the colporteurs what had happened. "I am here today," he said, "and not buried dead in the ground because of the Word of God. I read the Book to those hardened bandits, and they listened to the truths of the Bible and set me free. It is good to know God's truth. I am so very thankful for it."

And so it is today. God's Word is still the most valuable thing in the world. And who knows, someday your life may depend upon your knowledge of it.

---

*A colporteur is someone who shares God's truth by going door-to-door and selling Christian books.

8

Comfort and
the Robber

by Edgar A. Warren

For some time Comfort had been attending the mission school in West Africa. She had learned how to cook, how to sew, how to do simple arithmetic, and many other wonderful things. But best of all, she had learned about Jesus, His gift of salvation, and how to pray to God.

"If you are ever in difficulty or danger," the missionary had told the class, "pray to Jesus, and He will help you." To show what he meant, the teacher had told them how God had delivered Daniel in his hour of need, and how the prison doors had opened for Paul and Silas.

How wonderful! thought Comfort. *But they were great and good men. Would God do the same for me if I needed help?*

Now those happy school days were over. Comfort

was working as a traveling trader, selling small items from village to village. When her stock of goods were sold, she put all the money into her purse and went back to the big town to buy more things to sell. Then off she would go again.

On this particular day Comfort had sold everything. She was thankful that God had blessed her. And as a result she had an unusually large amount of money in the long leaf roll that she used as a purse. After the manner of her tribe, she put the roll under the folds of her brightly colored dress, where no one could see it. Then she made her way toward the big town.

Her way led along a narrow jungle path, and as she walked she began to sing some of the hymns she had learned at the mission school. Suddenly she saw something that made her heart skip a beat. She stopped singing. Coming along the path toward her was a rough-looking man. The path was too narrow for her to step out of his way.

He stopped her. "You've got money," he said sharply. "I want it. Give it to me!"

Comfort looked around. Was there no one to help her?

"Come on, now, take those things off. I'm in a hurry, and I must have that money. How much do you have, anyway?"

"Not very much," she faltered. "It wouldn't be much to you, but it's everything to me. If you take it, was the high wall that separated the wealthy home from the mission compound. On the second floor of the rich house, close to the wall, was a balcony. Mother, Father, and Johnny could see several men standing there fighting.

"What are they fighting for?" Mother asked.

"I think it's a thief, a burglar!" Father said.

Johnny's eyes grew big with excitement. A real live burglar?

The night watchman continued to blow his whistle to bring the police he knew were patrolling somewhere nearby. Ali, the mission gardener, ran around to the wall to keep the thief from coming over the wall into the mission compound.

The thief broke away from the servants, swung over the iron railing, and dropped to the concrete terrace below. Right after him came the servants. The thief ran into the garden. The servants were right behind him, shouting.

At the back of the garden was a greenhouse, and it was for this that the thief was heading. He hoped to get away by climbing onto the top of the greenhouse and dropping down over the wall beyond.

About this time two policemen rushed into the garden, shouting to the thief to stop! The thief kept right on going. Up on the greenhouse he climbed. Crash! One foot broke through the glass. Crash! Another foot went through the glass. The policemen started shooting. What a racket! Glass breaking, guns firing, and a woman next door on the other side of the mission shouting, "Police! Police!"

Suddenly all was quiet. Johnny strained his eyes to see if the police had caught the thief. "Have they got him?" he asked.

"I don't know yet," Father said. "I can't see them right now."

The group came back into the light. Sure enough, the thief was caught. His hands were tied tightly behind his back, and the police were leading him into the house.

When all the excitement was over, Johnny and his parents went back to their beds, but sleep was impossible. Johnny got out of bed and called down to the mission night watchman below. "What happened, Ali?"

The night watchman had been talking to the servants next door and knew the whole story. He told Johnny that the thief had had a master key, and had opened three doors before someone (possibly one of the servants) heard him. Apparently he was a professional thief, and was trying to leave himself an escape route. But he didn't have time to take anything before he was discovered.

"Why did he wait so late to break in?" Mother asked. "Didn't he know that people might be waking up at that time of the morning?" (It is usually quite light in other assorted items.

I was also carrying a handbag, which I admit was pretty big. When we had started the trip, I had one that I thought was pretty large. However, before the trip was half over, I bought another one more than twice its size. My new one was large enough to hold not only my former handbag but also a number of other small items I had added, among them a pair of wooden shoes from Holland, a cute Hummel figurine from Germany, a little glass bird from Italy, and most important of all, 10 film cartons containing 1,000 feet of color motion picture film. The film in my bag represented one fourth of our entire six weeks of work in Europe.

Once again we counted our luggage. They were all there.

While we were waiting for our flight, I wanted to change my dress for the trip, and my husband needed to rearrange some of his belongings, so we took our suitcases a few feet away to open them. If the terminal had been crowded, we would not have turned our backs even for a moment on the remainder of our things. But with almost no one around, we felt very confident. After all, those five bags were only a few feet away.

We did notice a woman, rather nicely dressed, standing on a stairway. About a minute later she passed between us and our luggage as we bent over our suitcases.

After finding the dress I wanted to wear, I headed for the women's restroom, leaving my husband with the bags. He soon finished repacking, and turning around, he noticed that my large handbag was missing. He concluded that I had it with me, and thought no more of it. Only when I returned 10 minutes later did we realize the awful truth: my bag with all its contents was gone.

The BOAC staff were very considerate, and the police were notified. They promised that they would do their best, but they pointed out that they didn't have a single clue to work with except the possibility that the thief was a woman.

We tried to assure ourselves that things could have been worse. Fortunately, both our passports were in my husband's pocket. In my handbag there was only $22 in cash, and the travelers' checks and other stolen items were not too important. But the 10 cartons of color film for Faith for Today, those were irreplaceable.

You can hardly imagine how terrible we felt as the plane carried us across the Atlantic to New York and home. We recalled the pictures we had taken of the grim tower in southern France where Marie Durant had been taken when she was only 15 years old, to remain until she was 52 because she refused to give up her faith. The lost footage included some taken in Prague, Czechoslovakia (now Czech Republic), where the brilliant young professor John Huss had preached the Reformation message back in the early 1400s. He paid with his life for his faith, but he is memorialized to this day by a large statue in Prague's old town square.

Some of the stolen footage also included shots taken in Wittenberg, Germany, where Martin Luther had nailed his 95 theses on the door, thus starting the Reformation in Germany. The book *The Great Controversy* had been our guide, describing Reformation times, and we were crushed that we wouldn't be able to use the pictures we had taken for the benefit of God's work.

Back at our office the next day we told the story to the dedicated Faith for Today workers. Everyone agreed that prayer was our only hope. The thief might very well have taken the cash and then dropped the bag and all its contents into the river Thames. The police had said it would be "like searching for a needle in a haystack," but we knew the Lord could help those films be found. Even though it seemed more hopeless with each passing day, our workers continued to pray.

After more than two weeks had gone by, I entered the First National City Bank near our office. One of the officials approached me. "Mrs. Fagal," she said, "the checks that were stolen from you in London have been returned." She handed me a small pad of our personal checks, which had been in the ill-fated handbag! She said they had been found in Victoria Station, a train depot near the air terminal. London's First National City Bank had forwarded the checks to our local branch.

Astonished and thrilled by this glimmer of hope, I immediately wrote to British Railways, thanking them for returning the checks, but telling them that our chief interest was in 10 cartons of film that had been in the same handbag with the checks. I also wrote to the BOAC staff, giving them all the new information we had.

For 12 days we heard nothing, and then things began to happen. An airmail letter arrived instructing us to go to New York's Kennedy Airport Cargo Building 66, where a package would be waiting for us. Once there, we hardly dared breathe as we cut the cords and slit open a 15-pound package revealing a large black zippered bag inside.

My hands trembled a bit as I unzipped it. There were the wooden shoes, the other handbag, and the great conglomeration of things that women usually carry. But we were interested only in the yellow cartons of movie film, which looked very beautiful to us just then. We counted them. Were all 10 there? Indeed they were—not one was missing. All that had been taken was the cash and an inexpensive old watch.

The thief had done exactly what we thought she would. She had removed what she wanted and then discarded the rest. But instead of dropping the bag in the river to hide her crime, she had left it in the railroad station where it could be found and held for someone to claim. Once again God's hand had been over His work in a truly marvelous way.

The Faith for Today films that were kept safe are already in use on the air, and the hearts of many are stirred as they watch the programs from week to week. Do we believe God answers prayers? Indeed we do. Again and again we have seen countless evidences that God's hand is guiding this television ministry. The case of the stolen handbag is just one more evidence.

---

*A Christian television ministry.

11

Robbers in My Church

by Sharon Titus

The abrupt entrance of two men through the swinging doors distracted the congregation from the sermon that Sabbath morning. Dressed in long, black trench coats and black hats, with nylon stockings pulled down over their faces, they stood silently at the rear of the church, each one holding a gun in ready position.

Glancing at our pastor standing at the pulpit and seeing the grim look on his face, we knew that this was for real. The two men were no ordinary visitors.

"What is it that you want?" inquired our pastor in a surprisingly controlled voice.

In clear, clipped words the order was given. "We want each of you to walk slowly, row by row, to the rear and drop your wallets in a pile on the floor."

All around the church people began slipping

of the telephone wires together, and in just a few minutes the police were swarming into the church. But the gunmen had made their getaway. After the police questioned us and searched for fingerprints and any other evidence, we were permitted to leave the church.

What an eventful Sabbath it was. We could see how God's protecting hand had been over us, and as we counted our blessings each of us thanked Him for His care.

Days went by, and it seemed that the robbery story had come to an end. Then one day something strange happened. As our pastor was sorting his mail, he picked up an envelope addressed in neat printing. He opened it and out fell a large sum of money. Quickly he read the enclosed note. Could it really be? Yes, he had read it correctly. It was from the gunmen who had robbed our church!

"We are sorry for all the trouble we caused you," the note said. "Please pray for us."

And pray we did!

12

Ingathering Bungles a Robbery

by Lois Zachary

Linda Williams stood on the corner of a shopping center in Nashville, Tennessee. It was mid-morning, and she and her academy friends were on their annual Ingathering* field day.

Linda looked at the leaflets in her hand. She had only two left, so she headed toward the parking area where Elder Don Holland, youth director, had parked his car. *Elder Holland is somewhere nearby and will have more papers for me*, she thought.

At that time of morning few people were around. The shopping center had opened only minutes before, and traffic was just beginning to flow into the area.

What was happening as Linda walked toward the parking area was something one reads about in newspapers and stories but is not something one wants to experience. Just across the street two men wearing ski masks and surgical gloves rushed out of the Third National Bank with a large cloth bag. What the two men didn't know was that an electrical current in the bank's door had activated a test gas bomb hidden among the $10,000 in bills. Seconds after they climbed into the getaway car, the bomb exploded. Fumes filled the car as a brightly colored dye began to spread over the money.

The men grabbed frantically for the money. They stuffed the bills in every available pocket and then fled their auto. Through smarting eyes they scanned the area for another possible getaway car.

While this was going on, Elder Holland had gotten the papers for Linda. He was just about to get back into his car when the two men jumped into it. Elder Holland had left the keys in his new blue-gray Renault. Running to the car, he grabbed the man behind the wheel by the shoulder and yelled, "Hey, man, you're stealing my car!"

Elder Holland stuck his head through the open window, only to come face to face with a .45 automatic. He had only a split second to decide what their intentions were and what he must do. Swiftly he dodged behind the small car, but how does one hide a six-foot frame behind a Renault?

While he was pondering his predicament, the robbers had problems of their own as they tried desperately to find reverse gear. And then, just as if it had been ordered, a police car came cruising down the street. Elder Holland dashed toward it shouting, "Those men are stealing my car!"

It was not a second too soon. The robbers found reverse gear just as the patrol car swerved in behind them.

"Watch out! Those men are armed," warned the pastor as the policemen approached the Renault. At this, they stepped back, pulled their guns, and gave a brisk order, "Get out of the car slowly, and put your hands on top."

In anger and defeat the robbers climbed out of the car. Their day was just not going well. They had not been able to pull off even robbery number one of the five they had planned for the day.

With a feeling of relief Elder Holland watched as the robbers were searched, handcuffed, and loaded into the back seat of the patrol car. Then he noticed the gun one of the policemen had confiscated. "That's not the gun that was pointed at me," he told the policemen. Quickly the robbers were ordered out of the car and searched again, but no gun was found.

By this time a crowd was gathering around the scene. Elder Holland, remembering the academy girls' purses in his car, went over to lock the door. There on the front floor board, among surgical gloves and ski masks, was the missing gun. In the back seat all mixed up with Ingathering leaflets was $10,000 in green bills.

That night when Linda returned to the academy, she had a very exciting experience to report. Breathlessly she recounted for her classmates the frightening events she had seen that morning.

"Weren't you scared?" they asked.

"Of course," answered Linda, "and all I could do to help was pray."

The gun the bandits had pointed at Elder Holland was loaded. One of the policemen opened the barrel and handed Elder Holland a bullet.

"Here," he said, "this could have been yours."

Holding the bullet, Elder Holland breathed a silent prayer of thanks for God's protection. His escape had indeed been a narrow one, for both men were high on drugs and one was on the FBI's most wanted list.

It was a happy day when Linda ran out of papers, but didn't run out of prayers.

---

*Ingathering is collecting donations to support the gospel mission of the church, often accompanied by handing out pamphlets.

13

Ministers to Bandits

by Barbara Westphal

Halt! Get off your horse! Hand me the reins!"
It was a holdup.

Angel, the teenage evangelist, had traveled alone on horseback three and a half days searching for a group of Sabbathkeepers deep in the mountains of Mexico.

"I organized a Sabbath school with 20 members," an active lay member had told him. "It takes several days to get there, but you must go and visit them. The place is a hideout for criminals. They live where the law can't find them."

Angel couldn't find them either. Somewhere he must have taken a wrong turn. He was lost, and now the armed bandit was making him dismount and demanding, "What's in your saddlebag?"

"A projector with reels and a battery adapter."

The bandit rummaged around in the leather bag and eyed the strange contraption. "Looks like a small cannon to me. What's it for?"

"It's to show pictures so that—"

"Come with me, and we'll see. If you're fooling me, I'll break your neck."

There was nothing to do but follow the bandit to his hideout. Angel mounted his horse again, but the bandit kept the reins and led him along a well-hidden path through the trees and rocks. For two hours they struggled down a steep canyon. When they reached the bottom, the bandit whistled. One by one, from behind trees, rough men appeared.

"What did you bring that fellow here for?" the leader complained.

"He says he has a picture outfit with him. If he doesn't, we'll kill him."

Both Angel and his horse were hungry, for they hadn't eaten all day, but the captain said, "It's dark enough to begin. We need some amusement, so let's get going."

As he set up the simple equipment, Angel remembered that he had only two light bulbs with him. He prayed that those bulbs, which often became overheated and broke, would last. He knew his life depended on pleasing the robber band.

What reel should he choose? Again he prayed. Then he selected the Plan of Salvation. He spoke straight from his heart about each picture. The script could be read in 35 minutes, but he talked on and on. He began to hear subdued exclamations from the hardened men.

"O God, have pity on me!"

"Forgive me!"

"What a miserable life I've lived!"

When he finally stopped, it was midnight. At last the captain said, "Are you hungry?"

They prepared a meal of beans and enchiladas, and after another hour they told him he could rest. But where?

"You sleep by me," ordered the gang leader. The bandit chief lay down on a bed and slipped his big machete and his .45 pistol under the blanket he used for a pillow. Under the bed was his Mauser (a rifle).

Angel knelt down and prayed before he lay down on the bed beside the thief. About 6:30 in the morning he woke up and found his horse, hoping to make a fast getaway. He was saddling when the others began to awaken.

"You mustn't go! You can't go!" they shouted. "You are our prisoner until you finish telling us about all the pictures you have."

They unsaddled his horse and led it away.

After a breakfast of hot tortillas the men sat down and Angel studied all morning with them. He showed another reel in the afternoon, and that night between

8:00 p.m. and 1:00 a.m. he presented two more.

The next morning he attempted to ride away again, but it was no use. They kept him with them for three days and four nights.

"Now you can go if you promise not to tell the authorities about us."

They sent one of their men as a guide. As they rode along together for seven hours, Angel talked to the bandit about changing his life and becoming a Christian. How happy he felt when the man said, "Be sure the seed you have sown will bear fruit in my life at least, if not in the lives of the others. I am going to leave the gang and start a new life."

He lovingly touched the Bible that Angel gave him, then he set him on the road toward the village that he had been looking for before his capture. At the parting of the ways the bandit asked, "When will you return?"

"I'll come through Huahatla again in three or four months," the evangelist promised. They knelt down and prayed together, then put their arms around each other in a tearful embrace.

"I'll change my life and will meet you again," were the last words of his guide.

Angel found the little Sabbath school group for which he had been searching and stayed a few days to give them special instruction.

Exactly four months later he returned to

Huahatla, wondering if he would find his bandit friend again. He was there, but how different! Angel scarcely recognized him. Not only were his clothes different—neat and clean—but his face was happy and honest instead of dark and fierce. He had studied the Bible and the lessons Angel had given him, and he was ready to be baptized. He had gone back to his wife and children and was eager to tell the gospel story to others.

Angel is now a pastor in Mexico City. He says, "What a providence it was that I lost my way and was a prisoner of bandits!"

14

The Missing Bible

by Judi Stafford Holt

He's threatened to kill you, Grimez. You'd better be careful!" Samuel said to the tall, broad-shouldered forester.

Grimez smiled at his companion and continued through the woods. "Samuel, you sound just like my wife, and I'll tell you the same thing I tell her. I've got my guns and my dogs. I don't need to worry." And with a scornful laugh Grimez turned down the path leading to his cabin.

In the unsettled days of the Napoleonic wars, Grimez and his wife, Maria, lived in a log cabin deep in the forest. Grimez was keeper of a large tract of woodland in the Silesian mountains. He had helped bring to justice a band of thieves and outlaws. Only their leader was still at large, and it was this leader who had sworn to have his revenge against the forester.

Maria was a Christian. She faithfully read her Bible and prayed. But Grimez seemed as irreligious as his wife was devout. He laughed at Maria and her prayers for his safety. "Don't waste your time praying for me, Maria, for I can certainly take care of myself. All I need is my gun and dogs, not your silly prayers!" But Maria continued to pray for him, asking God to protect him from the outlaw.

One evening Grimez did not come home at the usual time. As the night wore on, Maria became more and more anxious. She couldn't help remembering how the robber had sworn to take her husband's life. Finally she decided to go ahead and have worship with her mother and young daughter in spite of her fears. She would place her trust in the Lord for her husband's safety.

Picking up the large Bible, Maria read aloud from the seventy-first psalm: "In you, O Lord, I have taken refuge. . . . Be my rock of refuge. . . . Deliver me, O my God, from the hand of the wicked, from the grasp of evil and cruel men."

Then the three knelt together and Maria prayed. "Dear Lord, You know Grimez is a proud, yet good man, and You know how much we need him. Help him to put his trust in You. Keep him from danger. And Father, also bless the robber whom we fear. Have mercy on him, and soften his heart. Thank You for hearing our prayer! Amen."

Just as she finished tucking her daughter into bed, Maria heard footsteps on the path outside! Someone began pounding on the door!

"Maria, Maria! It's me, Grimez. Let me in!"

She ran to the door. "Oh, Grimez! How thankful I am that you're home safely! I've been so worried, and we had prayer for you."

"Bah," replied Grimez. "It's foolish to waste your time praying for me. Instead, you had better pray that my gun works and that my dogs are alert. That might do some good!"

Grimez shuttered and fastened each window, bolted the door, and checked his firearms before going to bed. All was safe and secure in the little cabin.

The next morning as the sun was just beginning to filter through the trees, Grimez got up to build the morning fire. To his great surprise, one of the front windows stood wide open! Then he noticed that Maria's large Bible, which she always left on the table, had disappeared. In its place was a sharp, dangerous-looking knife!

"I don't understand it," puzzled Grimez. "I double-checked those windows last night. I'm positive they were latched."

Obviously someone who had planned murder had been inside the cabin. Everyone searched the house, but they found nothing missing except the Bible.

Even Grimez had to admit that it was neither his guns nor his dogs that had saved his life.

Grimez thought about Maria's Bible during the next few days. He stopped laughing at his wife and gradually began to believe that there might be something to her prayers after all.

After that night the outlaw who had promised to kill Grimez simply disappeared. No one heard from him again.

Some years later war broke out, and Grimez enlisted in the army. He soon found himself on the front lines of battle where the fighting raged along a stretch of lake shore, deserted except for some little huts at the water's edge.

During the battle Grimez was shot. He felt a piercing pain in his side. Everything whirled, then turned black. When he came to, he was lying on the cold ground, the pain so bad that he couldn't move. The battle had moved on.

A little while later a fisherman rowed cautiously toward the shore to see whether his hut had been destroyed in the fighting. Hearing the groans of a wounded soldier, he landed and went to help him. "Over here," he called to his companions. "This one is still alive."

They carried the wounded man to their boat and rowed to the opposite shore of the lake, about two miles away. Here several cottages lay scattered along

"For weeks I hid in the woods near your home and did practically nothing but read your Bible. I saw what a great sinner I was, and like the other thief, the one on the cross, I was forgiven. Then I left that part of the country and became a fisherman.

"You, Grimez, trusted your guns and dogs, but they couldn't have helped you. God's Word saved you. It protected you then, and it also saved you on the battlefield. So don't thank me. Thank God, who through this blessed Book saved you—and me."

15

God Cares About Bicycles

by Goldie Down

At every step dust rose in suffocating clouds. It stuck to the boys' dark hair, their skin, their clothes, their books—everything wore a filmy coating of gray. Only their faces showed brown streaks where sweat had trickled down and washed away the dust.

"It's sure hot," Saraj sighed. "I wish we didn't have to make this walk in the hottest part of the day."

Daniel had to swallow twice to get the dust out of his mouth before he could reply. "I wish Kokergill village wasn't so far away. Nine miles is a long way to walk."

"I wish I could have a drink of water right now. I'm so thirsty."

"I wish we had bicycles. It wouldn't seem nearly so far if we could ride."

"I wish—" Saraj cut short his sentence, and the

dusty mask of his face cracked as he grinned. "What's the use of wishing? A bicycle would cost more than two months' wages, and neither of us can afford that."

Daniel nodded, blinking his eyes as a slight breeze blew up a fresh cloud of dust. "It would be much easier if we had bicycles, but I wouldn't miss this branch Sabbath school for anything. We're the only ones who can read the Bible to the villagers. They'll never hear the Bible stories unless we tell them."

"That's right." Saraj lengthened his stride in order to cover ground more quickly. "We're fortunate to be studying at a Seventh-day Adventist school, and we must share our faith."

Sabbath after Sabbath slipped rapidly by. Still there was heat, and still there was dust. (No matter what the season, the weather changes little in that part of Pakistan.)

One Tuesday afternoon Saraj was studying in the dormitory when Daniel rushed in. He was breathing hard from his run and was so excited that his words came tumbling out in unfinished sentences. "Our wishes have come true . . . school has bought bicycles . . . village evangelism . . . we can ride . . . no walk next Sabbath."

Saraj leaped to his feet, and the two of them jumped up and down for joy.

How important the boys felt the next Sabbath afternoon as they set out on the shiny new bicycles.

"Take care of those bicycles," the teacher in charge of lay activities warned. "They cost a lot of money, and we don't want any fooling around when they're ridden. They're for missionary activities only. No racing and chasing or—"

But Daniel and Saraj were already on their way. The teacher smiled as he looked after the cloud of gray dust that hung in the hot, still air, marking the route they had taken.

"Oh, well, they're good boys," he said. "I know they'll take care."

And take care they did. With their Bibles and lesson quarterlies tucked into cloth bags slung around their necks, the two boys hung onto the handle bars, grimly scanning the trail ahead to avoid running into stones and bumps and thorny bushes. In no way must these precious bicycles be scratched or injured.

How much quicker it was to ride than to walk. It seemed no time at all before they had reached Kokergill village. Nearly everyone turned out to admire the bicycles and to listen to the Bible stories. It was a good meeting, and the boys were happy as they mounted for the return journey.

For a mile or two the trail followed the line of the irrigation canal, and the boys had to watch carefully lest they swerve too far to the side and go hurtling down the steep bank and into the canal. They hadn't ridden far when a horseman appeared over the high embankment in front of them. Two more men, armed with guns, sprang up beside him.

"Stop!" they yelled.

Daniel, who was in front, stopped. Saraj had been lagging a little behind, and as soon as he saw the horseman appear he sensed trouble. Before anyone realized what was happening he turned his bicycle on the narrow trail and sped back toward the village.

"Where are you going?" the horseman demanded of Daniel.

Daniel was terrified. He knew these men must be *dacoits*—thieves who valued the lives of others as little as they valued the law.

"I'm taking this bicycle back to the Adventist school," Daniel stammered. "It's not mine. I only borrowed it."

The man laughed coarsely. "I'll say it's not yours. From now on that's my bicycle."

"Oh, no." Suddenly Daniel felt brave. He must protect what belonged to God and the school. With a prayer in his heart he said, "Please don't take this bicycle. It's used for missionary work. It belongs to God. You can't take it."

"Oh, can't I?" snapped the man angrily, leveling his gun at Daniel's chest. "If I shoot you, I can have it."

Quickly Daniel lifted his Bible and held it over his heart. "This is God's Book. It's a holy book like your Moslem Koran. God wouldn't like it if you shot me through His holy book."

For a few seconds the horseman hesitated. He believed in God even though he didn't obey His laws. Then one of the other men grabbed the bicycle. Beating Daniel about the head with the butt of his rifle he threw him to the ground.

"Get going, youngster," he yelled. "Run for your life before we kill you."

The men fired shots above Daniel's head and roared with laughter as he scuttled for cover.

"Keep going, kid," yelled the man, and a fresh burst of gunfire sent geysers of dust spouting into the air.

Daniel kept going. He didn't stop running until he reached Kokergill village, where Saraj was waiting for him.

"What will I do?" he cried as he collapsed outside one of the houses. "They took the bicycle I was riding. I tried my best to save it, but they—"

"I heard shots. Did they hit you?"

"No, but they stole the bicycle. What will the principal say? How can I go back to school and face him?"

"You did your best to save it," comforted Saraj. "Come on, we'd better go back and tell them what happened. I'll leave my bicycle here in case those fellows are still around. One of the villagers is hiding it for me."

The nine miles had never seemed so long as the discouraged boys trudged wearily back to school. When they told the principal their story he called the police, but there was nothing they could do. Many bands of *dacoits* roamed the countryside, and it was impossible to find their hideouts. The bicycle was gone and that was that.

Before sunrise the next morning Daniel again set out for Kokergill village. Saraj was working, so Daniel had agreed to go and bring the other bicycle back to the school.

As he jogged through the dust, discouraging questions kept racing through his mind. Why had God let this happen to the bicycle? It was being used for missionary work, wasn't that a good thing? Then why hadn't God looked after it? It would be a long time before the school would be able to purchase another one. Once again he and Saraj would have to take that long walk every Sabbath afternoon. Daniel sighed aloud. It had been so much quicker to ride. Maybe God had a reason, but it was hard to explain that to the villagers who were slowly learning to have faith in the God of heaven.

As he neared the embankment where the robbers had hidden, Daniel felt impressed to look down into the canal.

He shrugged off the feeling. *No, I'd better hurry on.*

Again the impression came that he should look

over the canal bank.

Daniel halted. For a split second he hesitated, and then he knelt on the edge of the trail and looked down at the canal. No one was in sight, and nothing was unusual. The water was flowing swift and deep between the reedy banks. Birds were stirring in their nests among the reeds.

Daniel was about to stand up and be on his way when a patch of white at the water's edge caught his eye. What was that?

He leaned as far forward as he could and looked more closely. There was a white cloth floating—and a bicycle. There was a bicycle lying in the water!

Excitedly Daniel clambered down the bank and pushed the reeds aside. Stretching as far as possible he managed to hook his fingers through the back wheel of the bicycle, and little by little he drew it toward him. It was a brand-new bicycle like the one he had ridden. Could it be the same one? Yes, there was the same brand name. It was the bicycle—God's bicycle—there was no doubt about it. But why had the robbers left it here?

As he pulled the bicycle out of the water, Daniel saw that the long white cloth was tangled in the chain. "Ah," he said aloud. The picture was clear to him now. One of the gunmen had mounted the bicycle, and the flowing end of his turban had become entangled in the cycle chain. Rather than take time to free it and risk being caught if Daniel had raised an alarm, the thief had hidden the bicycle among the reeds and escaped on foot.

He'll be back soon to collect it while it's early morning and not many people are about, thought Daniel as he worked frantically to tear the cloth out without breaking the chain. I must get to the village as fast as I can.

Tugging and twisting this way and that he finally freed the cloth, rolled it into a ball, and tucked it into his shirt. With great effort he managed to drag the cycle up the steep embankment and onto the road. As fast as he could he pedaled to Kokergill village.

The villagers were surprised to see him so early in the morning. They were even more surprised when they saw the bicycle and heard his story. Everyone gathered around and gazed in awe at the bicycle that had been so miraculously found.

"God saved it." The village elder stroked his bearded chin wisely. "God saved His bicycle. It's a miracle to get back something that has been stolen by *dacoits*. Your God is very great."

16

Betty's Bandits

by Jeannie McReynolds

In the warm sunlight a buggy clattered noisily over the "corduroy" road. Formed by laying logs crosswise side by side, it reminded Betty of the old washboard on which she scrubbed her clothes.

Buggies didn't have very good springs, and every bump seemed to jolt clear through her. But traveling along the bumpy road was better than sinking axle-deep into the mud on either side. The swamp was not a pleasant place, and the heat seemed to be increasing by the minute.

If she could just make all the deliveries today and collect the money for the books that had been ordered, she could pay her expenses for a few weeks while she took more orders in another community. There were easier ways to make a living—selling books door-to-door was lonely work sometimes—but to Betty, the joy of selling Christian books was sharing with others the precious blessings that meant so much to her. It was a thrill to find people who were interested in the Bible, those who would listen to her as she opened God's Word to them.

It was midmorning when Betty rode into the little farming community of Hansen. She hurried to one house after another, delivering books and collecting money.

The day wore away. Betty stopped under the shade of an old oak to eat her lunch, then with a quick glance at the sun, hurried back to her work. Surely she would be able to finish her deliveries today. The thought of resting at home with her sister, Helen, instead of riding the long, hot miles again the next day made her feet fly.

But then she arrived at the Thompsons' house. After two minutes' conversation, Betty knew she couldn't simply make the delivery and leave. Mary Thompson clung to Betty's hand, telling her of the terrible sickness that had stricken her husband. She needed comfort, she needed hope, she needed Jesus.

Betty sat for two hours on the faded sofa, turning to text after text and sharing the wonderful story of what Jesus had done in her own life. With tears of sympathy in her eyes she knelt beside the discouraged woman, pointing her to a loving Savior. Again and again she repeated the promises of God. Before she left, the clouds on Mary's face lifted and the sunshine of hope and joy came through.

With her heart singing, Betty ran down the steps and pulled the old gate shut behind her. Then she stopped short. The sun was sinking toward the western horizon. She would have to drive home in the dark. She pushed back the lump of fear rising in her throat. Everyone knew there were bandits on these roads at night. Uneasily she felt her lumpy purse, heavy with the money she had collected.

There were still 11 houses on her list. No way to avoid the long drive back the next day. She climbed into her little buggy and headed for home.

Night was already falling as she urged her horse along the narrow street that led out of the village. Betty had never been so frightened in all her experience selling books.

As she neared a fork in the road, she stopped the horse so she could think for a moment. Both roads led home. One went through the hills, and the other through the woodland swamp, the way she had come in the morning. The swamp road would be infested with a million mosquitoes, but it was more direct. If only she knew which way was safer! Silently she prayed for guidance and protection.

Suddenly her horse leaped forward and took off down the road through the swamp. Bumpity-bump, bumpity-bump, the buggy clattered over the corduroy road.

"Tom! Tom!" she called and pulled on the reins. The old gelding ignored her and continued his vigorous trot in the direction of home. Strange, she thought, hardly his usual behavior. She could only pray that God was guiding.

The prayer left her feeling better. She began singing softly: "Lonely? no, not lonely while Jesus standeth by; His presence always cheers me; I know that He is nigh." She could feel her courage oozing back. "No, never alone, no, never alone." Why should she be afraid with the King of the universe as her protector? Was she not on His business? Peace flowed through her heart.

In spite of the jolting, Betty had almost dozed off when Tom slowed and then stopped. She sat upright with a cold chill running down her back. Goose bumps stood on her arms, and she froze, not even breathing. There on the road in front of her was a large carriage carrying two men.

Why would two men be sitting out here on this lonely road at night? They could be up to no good! She was certain that they were waiting for her. Quietly she watched to see what they would do, every breath a prayer. They didn't move. They were facing the other direction. They didn't even turn their heads.

Still their carriage blocked the narrow road so completely that it was useless to think of trying to get by. It would be difficult even to turn around. What if she drove off the road? She craned her head to look. Even in the dim moonlight she could see the soft mud on either side that not even the horse could wade through. She cried silently to God, her mighty Protector.

A movement on the right caught her eye. Turning her head quickly, she gasped. A man was walking out of the woods. Even in the darkness his clothes were a white that reflected every gleam of light. He seemed to have no difficulty with the mud, but walked directly to where old Tom was standing.

Taking the bridle in his hand, he led the horse out onto the mud. Tom stepped along, drawing the buggy after him. The sticky marsh could just as well have been a paved highway. Around the big carriage and back up onto the road the man led them. Then, as the stranger gave Tom's flanks a sharp pat, the horse went flying down the road. Betty could only hang on.

Back at home Helen watched uneasily for her sister's return. A nagging feeling in her heart grew ever stronger that all was not well. The conviction remained that Betty was in danger, and she prayed for her sister's safety.

After what seemed hours Helen heard the sound of Tom's hooves on the driveway. Hurrying out, she saw him lathered and drooping with exhaustion.

Wordlessly she hugged Betty, a prayer of relief and thanksgiving in her heart.

"Come in," she said. "Tell me all about it."

The next morning, after finishing her deliveries, Betty felt an urge to visit the Thompsons. Mary met her at the door with a strange look on her face. "Where did you stay last night, Betty?" she asked.

"I went home," Betty answered, puzzled.

"Which road did you take?" Mary persisted. Betty told her.

When Betty told her, the older woman said, "I was really worried about you. After you left yesterday, we heard that there were bandits waiting for you on both roads."

Betty stood gazing at her, her eyes brimming with tears. "The angel of the Lord encamps around those who fear him, and he delivers them [Psalm 34:7]," she said quietly.

17

A Thief in the Night

by Arlene M. Smith

B *ang! Ploppety-plop-plop!*

"What happened?" shouted students as the bus jerked to a stop along the side of the road.

"It's a flat tire," replied the bus driver. "Just sit still and be calm while I try to get hold of someone back at the school."

It would have to happen tonight! I told myself. Our family was planning on going to the annual Open House at Glenview Junior Academy, and I would have gotten home just in time as it was. Now that we had a flat tire, I was bound to be late.

My thoughts were suddenly interrupted by the bus driver's announcement. "I've contacted the school, and they're sending us another bus. It should be here in about 15 minutes."

After what seemed like hours the spare bus arrived. Everyone transferred to it, and we were on our way once more. The time was 7:00 p.m., and I still had a good 25-minute ride before the bus would reach my stop. I wondered if Mom and Dad were waiting for me, or if I would have to stay home by myself.

When the bus finally arrived at my stop, I leaped off and headed for home as fast as I could. Bounding through the door into the house, I met Mom and Dad just as they were getting ready to leave. After I gave a quick explanation about what had happened, Dad said, "You can drive us over to the school and then come back and get ready to go. You won't miss too much of the program if you hurry."

I drove Mom and Dad over to the school, hurried back home, changed my clothes, locked up the house, and headed for the school again. I didn't know till later that two or three men were sitting in a van near our house watching me come and go.

Open House was especially good. But when the evening's activities were finally over I breathed a sigh of relief. I could now go home and relax after all the hustle and bustle of the past three and a half hours.

"Your dad and I are going to help clean things up," Mom said. "I know you have homework to do, so you can take the car home. When we're finished here, we'll call you, and you can come pick us up."

Living only six blocks away from the school proved to be a real advantage that night with all the trips we had to make back and forth. As I approached the house I noticed there was a light on in my room. I was sure I had turned it off when I left. Then as I started to pull into the driveway, I noticed the light in Mom and Dad's room come on. Shadows moved across the drapes. I thought at first that some friends must have dropped in, but how could they have gotten in without a key?

I sent up a quick prayer, "Lord, help me to make the right decision." Then I put the car in reverse and headed for the school.

After putting the car in park, I leaped out and ran to Dad. "Dad! Hurry! There's somebody in our house," I yelled.

Dropping the mop he had in his hands, Dad ran with me to the car. We jumped in and headed for home.

When we pulled into the driveway, the house was pitch black. "You stay here while I go see if anybody is still around," said Dad.

I sat in the car, watching him disappear through the gate into the backyard. I wondered if whoever had been in our house was still around. If so, I hoped and prayed they wouldn't hurt Dad.

Suddenly Dad yelled. Without a second thought I leaped out of the car and took off toward the backyard. I arrived in time to see Dad leap up on the fence as a van sped toward him then vanished down the alley.

"What happened?" I gasped as Dad came back into the yard.

"When I came around the corner a man was standing here by the gate to the alley. When he spotted me he yelled and took off running. I started to chase him, but then the van appeared. They tried to run me down, but I jumped onto the fence just in time."

"What did they do in the house?" I inquired.

"I don't know," said Dad, still trying to catch his breath. "Let's go take a look."

As we walked into the house, I froze in my tracks. What a mess! The refrigerator and freezer doors were standing wide open with food everywhere. Apples and oranges were all over the kitchen floor. The color television set in the family room was gone and Dad's radio was no longer on his desk. I looked up at Dad to see what he would say.

"Can you call the police while I go back to the school and get your mom?" he asked. "And be sure to keep the doors locked."

In no time Dad was back with Mom and we were waiting for the police to arrive. I decided to go look at my room. As I walked through the door, I could see that my stereo set and record albums were gone. Every drawer in my dresser had been pulled out and dumped in the middle of the floor. The mattresses and covers to the bed were on the other side of the room. All the dresses that had been in my closet were strewn everywhere.

A few minutes later the police arrived. They discovered that the thieves hadn't gotten away with a thing except $15 in cash. In the alley next to the fence was a pile of our belongings. Evidently the thieves were bringing the van around to the back to load everything up when we arrived on the scene.

Before I climbed into bed that night I thanked God for being with us. I also remembered the text in the Bible that tells us "the day of the Lord will come like a thief in the night" (1 Thessalonians 5:2). And I asked myself whether I was prepared to go and leave everything I owned behind, or was I getting too attached to my earthly possessions?

18

Grandma and the Bandits

by Judy Shull

In my grandmother's day, young women didn't travel unchaperoned around the countryside— most young women, that is. But my grandmother Ruth and her older sister, Bernice, were not like most.

The two sisters were attending school. Ruth planned to become a nurse, and Bernice was going to be a teacher. But now they were out of school for a few short weeks for summer break.

"I thought Michigan summers were hot, but this Florida heat is unbearable," Bernice said.

"Oh, don't complain," Ruth responded as she soaked her feet in a pan of cool water. "The winters are much easier here, and this heat isn't going to hurt us."

Neither sister said anything for a while, each lost in her own thoughts. Then Bernice hit the windowsill and excitedly walked across the room to where Ruth sat. "Let's take a week away from here and go to the ocean!"

"Ocean breezes sound good to me. Which way shall we go?" Ruth dried her feet on a towel and got up, ready to start packing right away. "Atlantic or Gulf of Mexico?"

"South," Bernice said.

"South? All the way south?"

"Yes, we've never been to the Florida Keys, so why don't we go?" Bernice's voice showed her excitement. "Look, we'll even get to go through the Everglades."

Ruth joined her sister, who was already studying the road map. "I don't know," she hesitated. "There's only one highway through the Everglades—and it isn't a well-traveled one."

"Good! No traffic. That will be nice. When shall we go?"

Ruth wasn't convinced. "But Bernice, what if we have a flat tire or trouble with the car in that area? No one will be around to help us."

"We'll just have to fix it ourselves then," Bernice replied, not the least concerned.

"I've heard that there are alligators in the ditches beside the highway. They might attack motorists who are stopped."

"Oh, Ruth, don't be such a worrier. We'll leave early enough to get through the Everglades before dark."

So a few days later the two sisters were on their way to the sunny Florida Keys. Ruth's worries disappeared as they rolled down the road in their shiny new car.

After traveling for a few hours, Bernice looked at her watch. "Ruth, I don't think we'll be through the Everglades before dark after all." She glanced worriedly at her sister and then at the rapidly sinking sun. Her heart raced as she pushed the gas pedal down farther. Although she felt confident of being able to fix a flat tire or a mechanical problem, being caught in the vast Everglades after dark raised goose bumps on her arms.

Dusk turned to darkness. The headlights reflected off the water in the ditch at the side of the road. Occasionally Bernice thought she saw eyes staring back at her. Shaking her head, she tried to assure herself that she was only imagining things. She prayed that she wouldn't have to stop by the roadside to fix anything.

The night breeze through the windows felt good, and soon Ruth fell into a light sleep. Suddenly Bernice stomped on the brakes so hard that Ruth flew forward, almost striking her head on the windshield.

In a shaking voice Bernice pointed ahead and quavered, "Ruth, what do you see?"

Ruth rubbed her eyes and looked. "Oh, Bernice, there are three men up there on the road!"

"One on the right and two on the left," Bernice observed. "What do you think they're doing? They have a chain stretched across the road!"

"Highway bandits!" Ruth gasped, fully realizing the danger they were in.

"I haven't seen another car for about an hour," Bernice remarked, trying not to let her sister know how scared she felt.

There was a giant swamp on either side of them, so they couldn't turn to the right or to the left. They couldn't turn around and go back, because they'd run out of gas before reaching a gas station.

"Those men will stop our car. They'll rob us and maybe hurt us, won't they?" The lump of fear in her throat made Ruth's voice faint.

"Yes, I believe that's what they have in mind. I don't know what to do."

"Let's pray!" Ruth promptly bowed her head and began a prayer for help.

"Ruth!" Bernice said excitedly. "There's a car behind us. See the headlights?"

"Where did it come from? We didn't see the car before, and we certainly would have seen headlights before now, since the land is so flat," Ruth reasoned.

"Look, the bandits see the car too, and they're dropping the chain. I guess they don't want to try to take two cars at once."

Bernice waited until the other car was right behind them. Then she stepped on the gas pedal and rushed past the outnumbered bandits.

Looking behind them, Ruth's eyes strained in the

darkness. "Bernice, I can't see the car behind us any-more. The headlights have just disappeared!"

Speechless with amazement and wonder, neither one of them said anything.

After they left the Everglades behind, Ruth spoke quietly. "What do you think we really saw when that car appeared and then disappeared?"

Bernice turned a radiant face toward her sister. "Ruth, I think we saw a car driven by our guardian angels from heaven."

19

The Man in Black

by Jessica Rumford

osa Rodriguez hummed quietly to herself as she ironed. Tonight it was quieter than usual because only the three Garcia children, whom she was baby-sitting, were home. She smiled as she heard 9-year-old Maria giggling in the back room with her little sisters, Evet and Marissa.

Rosa thought about how nice Mr. and Mrs. Garcia had been to her. When she had arrived in America a few months before, she had been without a job and didn't know the language. The Garcias had offered her a place to stay.

Suddenly her thoughts jolted to the present by a movement outside the window of their first floor apartment. Rosa squinted, trying to see better. She froze as she realized that a man was trying to cut through the window screen. For a moment that seemed like an eternity, Rosa was paralyzed with terror. All she could do was stare at the man dressed all in black, his knife glistening in the moonlight.

Rosa knew she must do something, but what? "Go away! I call police!" she yelled in her broken English.

But the man in black just looked at her and laughed.

"I call police!" she yelled again.

Again he only laughed and continued to cut the screen.

The girls! she thought frantically. *I must protect them.* Rosa ran back to their room. Good! The girls were there, safe.

Just then Marissa let out a scream as she stared out the window. Rosa followed her gaze. Directly outside their window stood the man in black, laughing as he continued cutting their window screen. Surely this was just a bad dream.

The girls began to cry, and Rosa spoke urgently in Spanish. "Get into bed, girls, and pray!"

Then Rosa grabbed a blanket and, with more courage than she believed she possessed, walked over to the window. Her pounding heart wiped out all other sounds. She threw the blanket over the window so they could no longer see the awful man.

"Girls, pray!" Rosa called as she ran out of the room to phone the police.

Once the call was made, a feeling of helplessness

washed over her. *There is nothing I can do,* she thought, pacing up and down the room. "Heavenly Father," she whispered, "protect us and keep us from all harm. Amen."

When the police came, she told them in her poor English what had happened. They searched the area but could not find the man. The only evidence of the intruder's night visit was the sliced screen.

Though he was never found, neither Rosa nor the girls ever forgot how the Lord had protected them that night from the man in black.

20

Break-in!

by Viva-Jane Haines

I stared in amazement at the large handprint that remained on the table where the television had sat. The print was twice as big as mine. What kind of person had entered our house and stolen the TV, videotape recorder, Dad's car keys, and who knows what else?

I felt very upset as I looked around the living room. I couldn't believe our home had been robbed. "Dear Jesus," I said as I closed my eyes, "help me to stay calm."

Mom was standing still in the middle of the room. She kept repeating, "We must be thankful that we're all safe."

I knew other homes in our neighborhood had been robbed, and some people had been hurt. I was thankful for God's care.

"But Mom," I pressed, "what about the missing car keys? What if the burglar comes back and steals our car?"

"Honey," Mom said, stroking my hair, "God will take care of the car keys somehow."

"I was up a half hour ago to get a drink of water," Dad said. "Then I went back to bed."

"How could this have happened in such a short time?" Mom wondered aloud. "I didn't hear a thing, did you?"

"No, at least not until just a few minutes ago. I guess I must've gone back to sleep soon after I went back to bed." Dad shook his head in disbelief. "The person or persons who did this must have been working on the windows while I was up! Why, it would have taken them some time just to get all the screws out."

"Dad, what should we do about the car?" I asked. "What if it gets stolen since they have the keys?" I felt especially worried because we lived a long way from town, where Mom and Dad worked at an Adventist hospital and where I went to school.

"I don't know right now," Dad assured me calmly, "but God will provide." We stood quietly while Dad prayed a prayer of thanks for our safety and that not many important things had been stolen.

"Do you see my wallet over there?" Dad walked over to the table, right next to the window where the burglars had come in. His eyes grew wide as he opened the wallet and flipped through hundreds of dollars. "I was paid yesterday for the whole month, and all the money is safely here. The fact that they didn't see the money is a miracle. And look! Here's my briefcase. It's full of personal things, and it's still here!"

Mom smiled. "You know, the truth is that we didn't actually use the TV or videotape recorder much. I'd say that all things considered, we are indeed blessed."

"But what about the car?" I pointed out.

"It's still in the driveway," Dad assured both Mom and me. "I guess I was awakened at just the right time."

I looked at the front door. It seemed so eerie with the paneled double doors standing wide open. I could feel a cool morning breeze blowing in. It was still dark outside, but Dad had turned on the porch lights as well as all the lights in the house.

"I guess they won't come back now that they know we're awake," I said as I glanced at Dad. "What should we do? It's still several hours before I need to get ready for school, but after having all this happen, I don't think I'll be able to sleep."

"Well, I'm going to check around some more," Dad informed us. "I'll keep watch on the place. Since we don't have a phone, at daybreak I'll have the neighbors call the police. Why don't you both lie back down and at least try to get some rest?" He then went outside to make certain that nothing was missing from the yard.

Mom and I sat down on the sofa. "Mom," I said as I rested my head on her arm, "Jesus really did take care of us, didn't He?"

"I'm sure of it," Mom said confidently.

Just then Dad came walking back in the front door. "Guess what I found," he said. He held up the keys to our car! "Looks like the burglars dropped them when they ran away. The keys were lying in the grass, and I spotted them as I waved my flashlight over the yard."

"Oh, thank You, Jesus, thank You!" we cried out. Now we wouldn't have to worry about someone walking around with the keys to our car.

"Well, Mom, we might as well rest if Dad's going to stay up," I said, suddenly feeling really tired. So Mom and I lay back down and slept for a few hours.

We were all up when the police came and took a look around. It was frightening to see the fingerprints the robbers had left behind, especially the great big one in the middle of the table. It was scary imagining what a person that size could have done to us. The police said we were lucky, but we knew it was more than luck. God had kept us safe.

21

Muddy Footprints

by Viva-Jane Haines

It had rained all night and part of the morning. Looking out through the rain-spotted window, I realized this was our chance. "Mom, the rain has stopped now. Shouldn't we go and check the Stewarts' home?"

"Yes, we should go before it starts raining again," Mom replied. "Put your boots and coat on. I'll get my things."

Mom went to the hall closet and grabbed her coat as I opened our front door. "I love the rain," I remarked. "It smells so fresh and clean."

"I do too," Mom agreed. "I'm glad it stopped, though, so we can check the Stewarts' home."

The Stewarts—out of town for a week—had asked us to check their house and get their mail while they were gone. As Mom and I crossed the street, we skipped over puddles and enjoyed the sight of rain-drops on the flowers. "Looks as if God gave all the plants a drink," I said with a laugh.

Crossing the big yard and driveway, we reached the Stewarts' front door. Out of habit, I rang the doorbell. "I'm used to doing that," I said with a grin. "Marilee always knows when I've come over to play."

Mom turned the key and pushed open the door. I entered the house and went straight into the living room while Mom stopped to pick up the newspaper on the floor. "Smells a little musty in here," she remarked. "I guess it's because of the rain."

"It sure is cold and dark," I agreed.

Just as Mom turned on the light, I noticed muddy footprints pressed into the white carpeting. A chill ran up and down my spine. "Mom, do I have mud on my boots?"

I put first one and then the other boot in the air for her to check.

"No," she answered, also noticing the muddy footprints. "Do I?"

When I shook my head no, Mom grabbed my hand and whispered, "I think we should go back home now."

Once we were back outside, Mom shut the front door and breathed a sigh of relief. "Honey, I think someone is in the house. The sliding glass door appeared to be open, and the footprints led from there to the bedrooms."

My head felt dizzy for a moment. "What, Mom?" I couldn't believe what she was saying.

Mom repeated it, adding, "We need to get help from the neighbors."

Running across the water-soaked lawn, we glanced toward the alley and noticed a black car. Two men were hurriedly opening the doors, getting ready to jump into the vehicle. We could see the Stewarts' TV stuffed in the trunk of the car.

We knocked loudly on the neighbor's door, but no one answered. We ran to the next house and knocked, but again no one answered. We rushed back home.

"Mom, we have to call the police right now!" My voice was trembling as Mom took in a deep breath.

"Thank You, Jesus, for watching over us," she said out loud as she dialed 911. Mom also called Dad, who promised to come right home.

The minutes seemed like hours as we sat on the couch. Mom and I knelt and thanked God for His protection. We knew we had been in the house with the burglars. We had walked so far into the house, they could have kidnapped us! Ringing the doorbell must have alerted them.

"I'm so thankful I prayed this morning for Jesus to be with me," I said.

"Yes, sweetie. I prayed for His protection too. In

fact, I read Hebrews 13:5, 6 during my prayer time. Let me get the Bible." Mom went into her bedroom and came back with the Bible. We sat closely together as Mom read, "'Never will I leave you; never will I forsake you.'"

I was relieved when I saw Dad drive up in his car. He walked in the front door and hugged us. "The police are over at the Stewarts' home," he said. "They want to talk to you both."

"Oh no, Dad," I moaned. "I can't go back over there. It's scary."

"The police have to know what happened," he gently replied. "I'll go with you."

This time it was raining as we trudged back to the Stewarts' house. Police cars were everywhere.

"Come in, please," one officer said. "We need to question you both on the robbery that took place here." It took more than an hour to tell the police officers the story.

The house looked terrible. The muddy footprints were all over the white carpeting. Many of the closets and drawers had been opened and searched through.

"You two are lucky," the police officer explained. "This wasn't the only home robbed. Four others in the same alleyway were too. The house you knocked on next door had burglars in it. You scared them away before they could steal much."

It took me several days to get over the scary feelings. When I shared my experience at Sabbath school, everyone was excited and thankful that Jesus had protected Mom and me. It's wonderful knowing He cares so much about us.

22

Banditos in Hiding

by E. C. Christie as told to Barbara Westphal

I am Captain Raymundo Benítez of the Mexican National Army." The words fell heavy upon the ears of the members gathered in the small Mexican church that Sabbath afternoon. The big captain, with his bronzed face marked by scars, firmly held their attention.

"Before I returned from the army I was very active in fighting the rebels up in the mountains," he continued. "Another duty I was given was to do all I could against the Protestants. I don't like to think about some of the horrible things I saw and did."

"Who is this captain?" a newcomer asked a church member.

"He is one of our church members who live up in the hills. They are sharing their experiences this afternoon."

"That's Delfín, all right!"

Forgetting about his wounds, José rushed through the brush with his friend to meet the lay preacher on the trail. Suddenly his friend realized something, and he blurted out the words to Delfín. "José was hit by six bullets. Look at his arm, his head, his cheek, his chest, and his stomach. But not a single bullet entered his body! The skin isn't even broken!"

As Delfín examined José, he found not what he might have expected—blood streaming from open wounds—but only six small bruises where the bullets had hit José's body and fallen harmlessly to the ground.

"God has taken care of you," Delfín asserted. "Now what?"

"We promised the Lord we would serve Him forever if He saved us. He did. But, Delfín, we need your help. We don't know what to do. The authorities will never believe we have changed. We can't come out of hiding."

"José, there is one person who can help you and get you out of your troubles with the authorities. He can also teach you the truths of the Adventist church. That man is Captain Raymundo Benítez."

"Who?" exclaimed both men in surprise. "You surely don't mean Captain Raymundo. He and his men used to hang the rebels from the nearest trees on the hillsides. We are probably the only two he wasn't able to catch. Not the captain!"

"Yes," Delfín answered quietly, "the captain can help you. He is a Christian now."

Finally the two men were persuaded to go to the captain. They came to him not with revolvers in their hands as in times past, but with the little red Bibles that Delfín had given them. And the captain met them, not sighting down the barrel of a high-powered rifle, but with a friendly handshake and a warm Mexican embrace.

23

Chasing Bandits

by Goldie M. Down

Harry rested his back against a box and made himself as comfortable as he could. He had to agree with Frank that traveling in a springless bullock cart with only a foot-high pile of straw to cushion one's bones was surely the most uncomfortable way of traveling in the world.

They had been traveling all day to take boxes of slates, chalk, and other supplies to one of the mission schools. Even with the best pair of bulls in this part of Burma, as Harry liked to boast, the going was slow, averaging only about two miles per hour. The trip would take four or five days.

About 3:00 a.m. Harry gave up trying to sleep. His entire body ached, and his stiff muscles rebelled against any further torture. Yawning, he looked around.

The half-moon had set about midnight, but the starlight was bright enough to throw the dark shapes of trees and bushes into silhouette against the sky.

The bulls looked gray and ghostly in the predawn twilight. Dew glistened on their shiny hides and curved horns. The slack nose ropes and Hteelun's bobbing head showed that their young driver slept.

Frank stirred, groaned, and rubbed his numbed limbs to restore circulation. "Are you awake?" he asked in a raspy voice.

"Yes, and I've had about as much of this cart as I can stand." Harry yawned again. "Why don't we get out and walk for a while? We can stride along, straighten out the kinks, and then sit by the side of the road and wait until Hteelun catches up."

"Great idea," Frank replied.

The two men clambered out of the cart, woke Hteelun, and told him their plan. Then they set off at a brisk walk.

Soon the creaking bullock cart fell far behind, and apart from their own voices, no sound marred the early-morning stillness. For more than two miles they kept up a steady pace, breathing deeply and enjoying the pure, clean air, free from the dust stirred up by the bulls' plodding hooves.

Around the next bend they saw a fallen tree conveniently near the trail, and Frank suggested that they rest awhile and wait for the cart. The two men sat on the log and talked about their mission work in Burma.

Suddenly Frank raised his head. "What's that noise?"

Both men turned their heads, listening intently to a faint sound in the distance. It grew louder. "Thakin Harry. Thakin. Thak—"

"It's Hteelun!" Harry leaped up and bolted back down the road with Frank at his heels. Why was the boy shouting? What could be wrong?

They pounded a quarter mile down the road before they saw Hteelun running toward them. Harry grabbed him by the arm. "What happened, Hteelun? Where's the cart?"

"Bandits, Thakin," the boy panted. "I was driving—quietly along—when four bandits suddenly sprang—out of the bushes alongside the road—and snatched the reins out of my hands. One of them held a knife over my head—while the others unyoked the bulls and drove them off into the bush. Thakin, I didn't know what to do—there were four of them—"

"It's all right, Hteelun," Harry soothed the frightened youth. "You couldn't do anything against so many. But we must get those bulls back. They'll slaughter them for food, and we can't let that happen."

The three hurried back to the abandoned cart, now tipped with its single shaft pointing skyward and its rear sunk into the dust. Nothing else had been taken.

Harry leaned over the side where his personal belongings were stacked and rustled around in the straw until he found the rifle that his friend, the forestry officer, had lent him to take on long trips.

Hteelun's eyes gleamed when he saw the big rifle, and the sight of the weapon seemed to put new courage into him. He feverishly ferreted around in the straw under a box of chalk and presently drew out his long dah-shey. Brave as a lion, now that he had the two missionaries to back him up, Hteelun waved the sword above his head.

"Which way did the bandits go?" Harry looked at Hteelun, and the boy swung his sword around to all points of the compass. "That way, Thakin, that way."

Harry shrugged, and started to prowl along the side of the road. Dawn's light and the four-feet-high grass trampled in one place beside the trail soon answered his question. He leaped forward and then paused to shout over his shoulder, "Frank, you'd better stay at the cart and guard our stuff. Hteelun, you go ahead of me. You can run faster than I can."

It was easy to follow the trail of trampled grass and bushes that gave way to soft dirt showing the bulls' tracks. The two ran steadily for nearly an hour before they came to a large clearing in the jungle. In the center of the clearing stood a solitary hut, built up on tall bamboo poles.

Hteelun was 50 or 60 paces ahead, and Harry heard him shout that he could see the stolen bulls tied to a post under the hut. He waved his sword menacingly above his head and dashed across the open area unmindful of the four bandits that Harry saw lolling on the hut veranda.

The bandits leaped to their feet, cursing and threatening the boy. But they made no move to rush down the ladder and overpower him, as they surely would have done if they had not spied Harry with his huge gun break cover and race toward them.

Harry's heart pounded madly, and not only from running. He knew something that none of the others knew—his gun was empty! He had forgotten to load it or bring any ammunition.

If the bandits suspected his gun was empty, Harry knew that they would not hesitate to kill him and Hteelun. Pausing in his advance, he raised his gun, opened the lock, pretended to load, and slammed it shut again with a great show and rattle.

Hteelun rushed under the hut and struggled to undo the knots that the captive bulls had drawn tight in their excited plunging and tossing. Harry continued to ran forward. He was halfway across the clearing when the bandit chief suddenly grabbed his swordlike dah-shey and sprang down the ladder, making straight toward him.

Harry went cold. What now? Had his bluff failed? He knew that these tribesmen could not only wield an expert sword but throw one with deadly accuracy.

Praying in his heart, Harry kept running forward.

The advancing bandit suddenly shouted in dialect, "My Lord!" Throwing his sword, handle first, in a gesture of surrender, he flung himself at Harry's feet.

Harry almost collapsed with relief, but he assumed a ferocious frown and rushed toward the bandit chief. "You villain!" Harry said boldly. "How dare you steal those bulls!"

The chief cowered still lower. "Oh, Thakin, I didn't know they belonged to you, or I wouldn't have done it!"

"But you did do it." Harry struggled to keep his voice stern. He felt sorry for the poor fellow cringing there in front of him. "It's lucky for you that those animals belong to me, a missionary. If I were a government officer, you'd be severely punished. But I am a man of God, and I love all men as brothers. Here—" Harry picked up the man's sword and held it out to him.

"No." The chief made no attempt to take it. "I am your slave."

Harry knew what he meant. According to Burmese custom, when two men met in combat the vanquished always became slave of the victor.

"No, no." Still leaving the sword on the ground

where the bandit might easily snatch it up and attack him, Harry held out his hand. "Let us be friends. What is your name?"

"They call me Dah-mya ["knife-thrower"]."

While the three bandits on the veranda gaped and muttered, Harry helped the chief to his feet. And the two of them walked, talking as they went, to the edge of the clearing, where Hteelun waited with the bulls.

24

Chicken Thief

by Judy MacDonnell

I wanted a pet. Not a cat, not a dog, but a white hen. So when my parents decided to order two dozen chicks from Australia, I was happy and excited. "You'll get to have your hen, plus the grown birds will provide eggs for the family," Dad had said. The order was mailed, and then we waited.

At that time we lived on a mission property called Bena Bena in the central highlands of New Guinea. My dad was the principal of the boarding school there, which was surrounded by rugged mountains. In some ways it was a lonely life for a missionary's kid. There were no other missionaries in the area, and I had to rely on correspondence lessons for my education.

The good thing was that we lived only about an hour away from the nearest town, Goroka. Other missionary families could go to their nearest town only once every six months, since they lived so far away. But we went once a week, even though traveling along the mountainous terrain was difficult.

One day, when we arrived in Goroka, there was a box waiting for us at the post office.

"Open it up," Dad said with a smile.

I didn't need further prompting. I carefully opened the box, and 25 pairs of bright little eyes blinked in the sudden light. The 25 fluffy chicks they belonged to huddled together.

With great excitement we took our chickens to their new home—a bamboo hut with a strong wire enclosure for them to run around in. They settled in quickly and began to grow. Weeks went by, and the baby birds became strong, healthy hens. We had no shortage of eggs.

But one morning when my dad went to let the hens out of the chicken house, he noticed that two were missing. There was nothing to be seen of them, not even a feather! That evening Dad carefully locked the gate.

A few days later two more chickens disappeared. This time Dad was really alarmed. At this rate it wouldn't be long before our flock was gone!

Dad put an extra wall inside the chickens' roosting house, but chickens disappeared anyhow. He tried setting up an alarm system, which would sound at the house if a thief broke into the pen, but it didn't work.

Then Dad thought of a new plan. He wrote down how much the chickens had cost and how much feed they had needed. He calculated how much the chickens were now worth, including eggs laid. Then he paid tithe on the "increase," or profit, we had potentially made on the flock.

"Dear heavenly Father," he prayed, "You have promised that if we bring all the tithes into the storehouse, You will rebuke the devourer. Please place Your hand over our chickens and protect them for us, if it is Your will. Amen."

The chickens were safe. They continued to provide us with a regular supply of fresh eggs, and no more chickens ever disappeared from the chicken house. We often wondered just how the Lord had stopped the chicken thief.

One day a student heard the villagers talking, and came to my dad with the story. "When you first brought the chickens here, two men were watching," he said. "One man lived in the village on the hill, and the other man lived in a village close by here.

"When the chickens were big enough to be eaten, the two men hid in the long grass and waited for you to lock up for the night. Then after dark they worked their way inside the pen, breaking through the thatch and wire until they could steal two chickens, one for each of them. Every few days they would come back and take another two.

"One day while they were hiding in the long grass, a tall man dressed in white clothes walked down the hill toward them. The tall man went past the chicken house directly to where the two men were hiding. One thief jumped up and ran toward the village. The other thief ran a long way and then hid in the long grass on top of a hill.

"The tall man in white followed the thief who ran up the hill. When he reached the place where the thief was hiding, the tall man leaned over and touched him. Then the tall man disappeared! The two men were so afraid that they decided they'd never steal your chickens again."

We knew that it was no ordinary man who had chased the thieves that night. The red dust of the highlands made it impossible to keep white clothing white!

That night my dad prayed a special prayer. "Thank You, Lord, for sending an angel to guard our chickens. We know that if You are concerned about the safety of our chickens, You must be even more concerned about the welfare of us, Your children!"

We've been curled.

Twirled.

Children can be so cruel.

Doodled on.

And telescoped.

Yet even when we feel persecuted, we know kids are learning about God, His goodness, and His grace. Our riveting stories, challenging puzzles, nature tales, and fun facts enthrall 10- to 14-year-olds with the gospel. Make sure your kids get their hands on *Guide* every week.

Guide. An invaluable resource for molding young minds. Even if it does get a little bent out of shape.

Now in Color!

See your Sabbath School secretary to order for your junior class. For home delivery, call **1-800-765-6955.**

www.guidemagazine.org